Go on all of Zac's missions in

#1 POISON ISLAND

#2 DEEP WATERS

#3 MIND GAMES

#4 FROZEN FEAR

POISON ISLAND
BY H. I. LARRY

ILLUSTRATIONS BY ASH OSWALD

SQUARE
FISH

FEIWEL AND FRIENDS
New York

With special thanks to the spies of
years 2 and 3 (2005) of the St. Michael's unit of GIB
for their top secret mission support.

SQUARE
FISH

An Imprint of Macmillan

Library of Congress Cataloging-in-Publication Data
Larry, H. I.
Poison island / by H. I. Larry ; illustrations by Ash Oswald.
p.   cm.   — (Zac Power)
Summary: Separated from his parents and older brother, twelve-year-old Zac,
a secret agent of the Government Investigation Bureau, must rely on his own skills
to obtain the formula for Dr. Drastic's secret Solution X.
ISBN 978-0-312-34659-1
[1. Spies—Fiction. 2. Adventure and adventurers—Fiction.] I. Oswald, Ash, ill. II. Title.
PZ7.L323783Poi 2008   [Fic]—dc22   2008034794

Originally published in Australia by Hardie Grant Egmont
Published in the United States by Feiwel and Friends
First Square Fish Edition: April 2012
Square Fish logo designed by Filomena Tuosto
Illustration and design by Ash Oswald
mackids.com

20   19   18   17   16   15   14   13   12

AR: 4.2 / F&P: O / LEXILE: 610L

CHAPTER ...ONE

If it were up to Zac, the Power family would have stayed right where they were, cruising in a jumbo jet 30,000 feet above the ocean.

Zac sat listening to his iPod with the sound turned up, finishing off his chocolate ice cream. The cabin was dark. Around him, everyone was dozing. It was as warm and cozy as naptime in kindergarten.

"Zac! Take off those headphones this minute and listen to me."

His mom's angry face appeared beside him in the darkness. She showed him the time on her chunky digital wristwatch.

Uh-oh.

"You were supposed to have your gear on three minutes ago," his mom said, half whispering and half yelling. "We can't afford mistakes at this stage of the mission, Zac."

Sighing, Zac reached under the seat for his backpack. He'd been having an excellent daydream about playing a guitar solo in front of thousands of fans. But there was no chance he'd be doing that anytime soon.

Instead, Zac slipped on his jumpsuit, goggles, and parachute.

Zac looked over at his brother, Leon. Leon was already changed and was busy tucking his favorite book, *The Manual of Advanced Electronic Gadgets (4th Edition)*, safely into his jumpsuit pocket.

Again, Zac wondered how he'd ended up with a big brother as geeky as Leon.

Zac's dad leaned over from the seat behind them.

"Nervous, Leon?" his dad asked.

Leon was shaking with fear already.

"What about you, Zac?" his dad asked.

As if he was worried! He was 12 years old now, and anyway, he'd done this kind of thing a million times before.

If anything, Zac was bored. What was the point of death-defying adventures if you had to keep them secret? His friends had no idea Zac was a spy for the Government Investigation Bureau (or GIB for short).

As far as they knew, Zac was away on

another boring old family vacation. There was nothing cool about that.

Anger bubbled up in Zac. He was just about to say something to his dad when he noticed a flight attendant walking toward him. She had a fake-looking smile on her face.

"Would you like a lollipop, *little boy?*" she asked.

Little boy! Zac's fists clenched.

"Come with me," she went on, "and I'll show you where they are."

The flight attendant pushed Zac toward the back of the plane and through some curtains. A bowl of lollipops sat on a counter. Zac took a red one, but the flight attendant slapped it out of his hand.

"No! The green one," she said, sounding tough now that they were alone.

Zac popped the green lollipop into his mouth. The sugar coating melted instantly, leaving behind a small disc on his tongue.

"It contains your mission," explained the flight attendant. "Guard it carefully."

Then she stepped on a square of carpet and a trapdoor popped open.

"Into the airlock," she ordered.

Zac stepped down into the dark space beneath the trapdoor. He straightened his goggles and ran his fingers through his dark brown hair. It flopped back into exactly the same place, the way it always did.

He was ready. The flight attendant silently counted down on her fingers.

...5
...4
...3
...2
...1
-

Zac took a flying leap out of the airlock and into the black night.

A split second later, Zac was falling at 200 miles an hour. Wind rushed past him. It roared in his ears. It sucked his cheeks back hard against his skull.

Zac tugged his rip cord and his parachute opened.

Whoosh!

His whole body jolted as he slowed to a drift.

Finally, Zac's sneakers slammed into the ground below. He'd found the drop zone. He fell clear of his chute and into a commando roll.

He got up and looked around. Where on earth was he? He didn't know what dangers would be waiting for him, or what kind of people he might meet on this mission.

Whoever they were, one thing was for sure—they wouldn't be looking forward to a friendly visit from Zac Power.

CHAPTER  ...TWO

It was hot, steamy, and very, very dark. Zac held his hand up in front of his face. Nothing. He couldn't even see an inch in front of him.

The darkness made the croaking of frogs and the angry buzzing of insects seem even louder. It was raining hard, and Zac was soaked already.

He felt in his pocket for his SpyPad.

The SpyPad looked a little like a video game, but was actually a mini computer, mobile satellite telephone with voice scrambler, laser, and code breaker all rolled into one.

Zac had the turbo deluxe model, which came with a color screen and real tone sound effects for the built-in games. But this was no time for games.

Zac spat out the disc the air hostess had given him and loaded it into his SpyPad.

...loading...

A message popped up on the screen:

CLASSIFIED

MISSION RECEIVED
SUNDAY 11:59 PM

The evil Dr. Drastic has invented
something called Solution X.
This is a cure for every type of disease
that has ever existed.
Sources tell us that Dr. Drastic is making
Solution X in a top secret laboratory
somewhere on Poison Island.

YOUR MISSION
- Find the secret lab.
- Secure the formula for Solution X.
- Return it safely to Mission Control
  before Monday 12:00 a.m.

END

  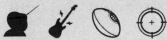

STUN GUN
>>> OFF

Suddenly, Zac heard a noise behind him.

THUNK!

He turned around.

Then he heard it again.

THUNK!
THUNK!

Somewhere to his right, Zac heard footsteps. A hand clapped him across the back.

"Rough landing, son?" his dad asked. "That was Agent Frost playing the flight attendant. Hopeless, didn't you think?"

Nothing about spying was ever easy or comfortable, in Zac's experience. He wished they could just get on with the mission. Then he could get home and practice more on his guitar.

His mom's serious voice cut through his thoughts like a knife.

"What are our orders, Zac?"

As Zac passed her the SpyPad, he heard a worried voice. "Mom? Dad? Zac?"

"Shhh, Leon! Anybody could be listening," said his mom, as she read the orders from Zac's SpyPad.

"OK. It's 1:21 a.m. That doesn't give us much time. I suggest we separate," said his dad.

Zac's mom consulted her wristwatch

compass. "OK, Zac, you and Leon head east to the center of the island." Then she added in a quiet voice just for Zac, "I'm counting on you to look out for Leon."

Zac rolled his eyes. His mom may as well have put handcuffs on him. Even though he was older, Leon was slow, scared, and a generally hopeless spy. Zac wished, just this once, he could finish a mission all by himself.

He'd *really* be a hero then.

"Your mom and I will search the coastline," his dad continued. "If you see anything suspicious, send us a message with your SpyPad."

As his parents left, Zac's mom whispered in his ear, "We're heading straight home after the mission. You've got to walk Espy." Espy, short for Espionage, was the family dog.

With that, his parents were gone. Zac and Leon were alone.

"Ready, Leon?" asked Zac gruffly.

"Um, Zac . . . I'm tangled in my parachute."

Zac sighed. It was going to be a very long mission.

Zac and Leon might have been walking through the jungle, but it felt like they were swimming in glue. Zac was hot and tired already, and they'd only been walking for an hour.

Dripping with sweat, Zac stopped to listen for the crunch of Leon's footsteps. But behind him, everything was silent. *Surely not even Leon could be lost already?*

Zac turned. There was Leon, a few steps back. He was standing with his head to one side, listening to something. His glasses were two round patches of steam.

"Listen, Zac," he whispered, out of breath.

"Who is it? Dr. Drastic?"

"No," said Leon. "Frogs."

Zac gave Leon his "Like I Care" face.

"Hundreds of them," Leon continued.

"And by the sound of it, they're dentro-bates!"

Zac grabbed Leon's arm. He almost ripped it from the socket.

"Let's just keep moving, OK?"

"Dentrobates, or poison dart frogs," said Leon in a huff, "have the most deadly poison of any known animal in the world.

DENTROBATE

aka
POISON DART FROG

DANGER!
Skin contains
a deadly poison.

DO NOT TOUCH!

Poisonous Skin

BEWARE

If you just *touch* one, it will paralyze or even kill you."

"Right. Whatever," said Zac, pretending he wasn't impressed.

They walked on in silence.

A few minutes later, something made Zac stop again. He had the creepy feeling that someone was watching them.

Then Zac heard a noise—it was so quiet he wasn't sure it was real.

There it was again! It sounded like leaves rustling. He hadn't imagined it.

Next, Zac heard a click and the soft whistling sound of something flying through the air.

"Did you hear that, Leon?" he whispered.

Silence.

"Leon?" he said again. "Are you OK?"

But Leon didn't answer. When Zac turned to look at him, Leon had the weirdest look on his face, like he was sleeping with his eyes open.

Leon wobbled unsteadily on his feet. He was going to collapse!

Zac saw something sticking out of Leon's back. A dart! That was what he'd heard whistling through the air.

Zac ran back. He braced himself for a **WHOOMP!** as his brother hit the ground.

But suddenly, a huge net fell from the trees above. Leon was tangled up like an insect in a spiderweb. Pulleys dragged the net up into the treetops again, taking Leon with them.

It's a booby trap! And the men firing the darts must be Dr. Drastic's henchmen. Is Leon dead or alive? Zac couldn't tell.

Zac's stomach twisted in knots. He was supposed to watch out for Leon, but now Dr. Drastic had him. He'd failed his parents. Even worse, Zac knew he'd failed GIB. Now that Leon was being held captive, Dr. Drastic would know that GIB agents were on the island, looking for his secret lab.

Whichever way you looked at it, Zac had blown the entire mission!

CHAPTER ... THREE

Zac had only been standing there, thinking those dreadful thoughts, for a few seconds. But it felt like hours. And it must have given Dr. Drastic's henchmen time to reload their dart guns because . . .

Ffftt!

Ffftt!

Ffftt!

A hail of darts shot through the darkness, straight toward Zac.

Zac knew exactly what he had to do. On his first day in spy school, Zac had learned an important lesson:

G·I·B

**WHATEVER HAPPENS,
A SPY MUST ALWAYS
COMPLETE THE MISSION.
THERE'S NO ROOM FOR SYMPATHY
AND NO ROOM FOR FEAR.**

He'd have to rescue Leon later. Right now, Zac had to run.

Dr. Drastic's henchmen were getting close.

"Sending two kids!" sneered one of them. "GIB must be getting desperate for spies."

Blood pounded angrily in Zac's head. *Kids! How dare they!*

He'd never moved so fast in all his life.

"Stop him!" yelled one of the henchmen. "He's getting away!"

The two henchmen raced through the jungle after Zac.

In the heat and panic, voices seemed to rush at Zac from all directions. Which way was forward? Which was up? Which was down? Was he going in circles?

It didn't matter.

He just had to get as far away from those voices as he could.

Zac had no idea how far he ran, or for how long. Eventually, he noticed the voices behind him fading until, finally, they were gone. He'd outrun Dr. Drastic's henchmen.

Hiding himself carefully behind a tree, Zac stopped at last. He had to decide what to do next.

He felt in the pocket of his cargo pants for his SpyPad. Yes, there it was. Safe and sound. He flicked it on.

He could call his parents, but that would mean telling them he'd lost Leon. He could call GIB, but then he'd have to admit he'd blown his cover. Zac imagined his mom's face as he told her Leon had fallen into one of Dr. Drastic's booby traps.

He punched in the secret number for GIB. The phone at Mission Control rang.

"This is GIB. Prepare for security clearance."

Zac held his SpyPad to his fingertip while it scanned his fingerprint.

"Hello, Zac," said a voice at Mission Control.

"Oh, hi," began Zac. "I—aahhhhhhhh!"

"Zac? Do you read me?" came the voice on the other end of the SpyPad.

But Zac couldn't hear it. He'd tripped on a tree root, stumbled forward, and let go of his SpyPad. As if in slow motion, the SpyPad was flying through the air. It hit a pitch of sandy ground, then, mysteriously, began to sink.

Oh no! thought Zac. *Quicksand!*

A spy must never be without a SpyPad. Zac had to get it back! He jumped into the quicksand, and right away his hands closed around the SpyPad. Yes! It was safe.

OK, thought Zac. *Now to get out of this quicksand. It can't be so hard. . . .*

He tried to lift his left leg out. But the quicksand moved underneath him like liquid. It sucked him down even lower!

He tried his right leg.

No luck! He was sinking fast.

Zac knew the best way to get out of quicksand: Stay still and wait for someone to come and pull you out. But no one except for Dr. Drastic's henchmen knew even roughly where he was.

An idea popped into Zac's head: *What if I let myself sink all the way through the quicksand until I reach solid ground at the bottom?*

Then he could use his official GIB Tramp-o-Socks to bounce his way out. Tramp-o-Socks were like ordinary sports socks, except each heel was fitted with an extra-springy miniature trampoline.

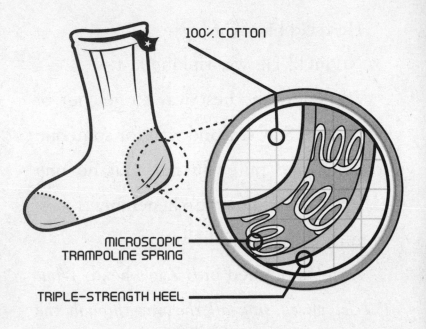

100% COTTON

MICROSCOPIC
TRAMPOLINE SPRING

TRIPLE-STRENGTH HEEL

Zac took a deep breath and dove into the quicksand. It swallowed him up with a . . . *GLUB* . . . *GLUB* . . . **GLUB**!

Zac wiggled off one sneaker, then the other. Even the slightest effort made him feel dizzy.

He was running out of air!

But just when Zac thought he couldn't hold his breath for a second longer, he hit solid ground. With all his might, he hurled his heels in their Tramp-o-Socks against the bottom.

Zac shot up, up, up through the quicksand and burst out through the top of it. He soared though the air, gasping for air as he flew.

THUD!

He landed heavily on solid rock.

He was right near the mouth of a cave.

CHAPTER ...FOUR

Zac crawled into the gloomy cave. Rocks cut his knees, but he didn't care. He was just too tired to stand up.

The cave smelled awful, like dead bats and sweaty armpits mixed together. Zac hardly noticed. A dark cave was the perfect place to hide for a while. Right now, that was all that mattered.

Feeling along the rocky cave walls, Zac

came to a ledge sticking out. Relieved, he crawled underneath and took out his SpyPad. The message light was blinking. Maybe someone at GIB knew he was in trouble and was sending backup!

MESSAGE RECEIVED 8:03 AM

Thieves have raided
Government Mint.
Millions of dollars stolen.
Agent Tool Belt (dad) and I
have been sent to investigate.
We're sure you and Leon can
handle Dr. Drastic yourselves.

Remember, it's your
turn to walk Espy. :)

MESSAGE FROM
AGENT TLC (MOM)

MESSAGE
>>> READ MODE

Water dripped on Zac's head. He shivered. Everything depended on him now. Just a couple of hours ago, Zac had been wishing he could finish a mission all by himself. Now that it was really happening, Zac wasn't sure he liked it after all.

Zac switched his SpyPad to Write Message mode. He needed to send GIB a full update. He was typing away when he heard a sound.

It sounded like footsteps!

Zac crouched down lower under the rock ledge. Yes, it was definitely footsteps, and they were coming his way.

He stayed statue still.

He hardly dared to breathe!

"How long's this gonna take, Bruce?" said a man's voice.

Zac listened closely. The voice was the same one he'd heard back in the jungle when Leon was captured. It seemed to come from farther inside the cave.

"As long as Dr. Drastic says, Bradley," said the second henchman.

What now? thought Zac.

He could make a break for it and run out of the cave. But he didn't like his chances of outrunning the henchmen twice in one day. Better to stay hidden. He might even learn something.

As though he'd read Zac's mind, Bradley piped up with a question.

"Anyway, what's Dr. Drastic got in that lab that's so important?" he said.

"You fool! It's the boss's biggest project ever! Solution X," said Bruce.

"Oh, yeah? And how's he make that?"

In his rocky hiding place, Zac turned red with excitement. This knucklehead was about to give him just the clue he needed to get the mission back on track!

"Seen those poison frogs everywhere? Well, the boss discovered if you boil their poison and add a few secret ingredients, you get Solution X."

"Wow," said Bradley.

Zac could tell that he didn't understand anything Bruce had said.

"It's gonna make the boss rich," said Bruce.

"So where do those little brats from GIB fit in?"

Brats! Zac wished he could shout back something really rude.

"Dr. Drastic told the world's governments he'll sell them Solution X if they pay one million dollars each within 24 hours. Guess they don't want to pay. GIB must've sent the kids to find the formula before time runs out and Dr. Drastic destroys it," sniffed Bruce.

Bradley sniggered. "Do they know he's gonna kill that nerdy Leon kid, too?" he asked.

Kill Leon? Zac shivered.

"Dunno, Bradley. All we have to worry about is keeping Solution X and the kid safely locked in the lab until the deadline passes," said Bruce.

"I'm sitting down then," said Bradley. "Bet we'll be guarding the lab entrance for a while. And I'm starving!"

The lab must be somewhere on the other side of Bruce and Bradley! Zac had to get past them, fast. But how?

Suddenly, Zac had an idea. It was risky, but things were really desperate now.

He turned his SpyPad to Voice Scrambling mode. He took a deep breath and shouted into the microphone. "Hot dogs!

Ice cream! Ice-cold drinks!"

The voice that came out didn't sound like Zac's voice at all.

It sounded exactly like a grown man selling snacks at a baseball stadium.

"Awwwright!" said Bradley greedily. "I could really go for a hot dog right now."

"Me, too!" said Bruce. "Didn't know there were snack vendors on the island though," he said thoughtfully.

"Me, neither. First time for everything, I guess!" Bradley said.

"French fries!" called Zac through the Voice Scrambler.

Bruce and Bradley stood up. They practically fell over each other to be first out of the cave.

"I'm getting a hot dog and french fries. Or maybe two hot dogs!" said Bruce, running.

"Do you think they'll have ketchup out here?" said Bradley, his voice fading into the distance.

Zac had done it! The cave was empty. Next stop—Dr. Drastic's secret lab.

CHAPTER ...FIVE

By now, Zac's eyes were used to the darkness inside the cave. He saw stalactites
hanging down from the roof like daggers.
Directly in front of him was a long, narrow
tunnel leading farther into the cave. That
had to be the way to the lab!

He set off along the passage. He ran,
but carefully. There was a stream running
along the floor of the tunnel, and the rocks

were slippery. He couldn't afford to fall and crack his head. Solution X and Leon would be lost for sure.

Then again, Zac didn't know how long Bruce and Bradley would wander the jungle looking for a snack vendor that didn't exist. Yes, they were dumb. But *how* dumb?

The deeper into the cave Zac went, the narrower the tunnel became. Soon he was on all fours, just barely squeezing through.

It got darker.

And colder.

And scarier.

If something happened to Zac down here, he knew he would never be found.

Just as soon as he thought this, the

rocky passage walls started to shake! Deep rumbling sounds came at him from every direction.

BOOM! BOOM! BOOM!

Rocks pelted down all around him. The passage was caving in! It was another one of Dr. Drastic's booby traps. Zac must have accidentally triggered a trip wire.

Zac tried to speed crawl forward along the tunnel. But a huge pile of rocks blocked his way. He crawled backward along the tunnel, only to find an even bigger pile of rocks there.

Zac was trapped.

He felt around in his pockets.

He needed something—anything!—
to dig with. But Zac had nothing but his
SpyPad, a roll of grape Bubble Tape with
hair stuck to it, and his iPod.

Wait—his iPod!

His dad was always telling him he had his
music up so loud it made the walls shake.

*Maybe I could force the rocks out of the way
by triggering another rock slide using sound
waves,* thought Zac.

There was always
the risk that even more
rocks would fall, but it
was his only chance.

Zac hooked his iPod
to his SpyPad.

His SpyPad had awesome built-in speakers. They were unbelievably powerful for something so small.

Zac checked the music on his iPod.

To trigger a rock slide, he'd need something really, really loud! He found his favorite song, "Torture Your Ears."

Perfect!

Zac set the volume to ten.

He blocked his ears and hit PLAY.

yelled the lead singer.

The force of the sound waves blew Zac across the tunnel. There was no word for it other than awesome. But best of all, the rocks blocking Zac's way forward had been blown apart! All that stood in his way now was a big pile of dust.

Zac got back down on all fours. He crawled deeper into the tunnel. The rock concert had been very cool, but there was no time to waste.

It was already 2:43 p.m.!

He must be getting close to Dr. Drastic's lab by now. And sure enough, the tunnel started to widen. The stream on the floor of the tunnel deepened. Soon, Zac was standing knee-deep in water.

He rounded a final bend. The tunnel ended in an enormous, rocky chamber. Zac found himself on the edge of a lake that took up most of the area.

He took a look around. *If this is the end of the tunnel*, thought Zac, *then the entrance to the secret lab must be somewhere in this rocky room.*

But where? All Zac could see were smooth, hard walls. No secret passages. No doors with codes to crack.

Absolutely nothing.

Then, in the darkness, Zac almost

tripped over something stuck into the shore of the lake. He got down low to have a good look.

It was a sign that said "No Fishing." Beside the writing was a picture of a fisherman looking alarmed as a fish with huge and bloody fangs chewed his arm right off.

It was a piranha!

Zac had seen a dead one once, on a mission in the Amazon. A piranha could chew all your skin off in ten minutes flat. But what would a fish that only lives in the Amazon be doing on Poison Island?

Unless . . .

Suddenly, Zac was certain. *The lab entrance must be right at the bottom of the lake, protected by Dr. Drastic's final booby trap!*

A piranha-infested lake!

CHAPTER ...SIX

In his mind, Zac made a list of things he'd need to dive into the piranha-infested lake.

First, a diving mask.

But he didn't have one.

Second, an oxygen tank. No, he didn't have one of those, either. GIB didn't think he'd need one in the middle of a jungle.

Third, a piranha-proof suit.

No, he'd left that at home, too.

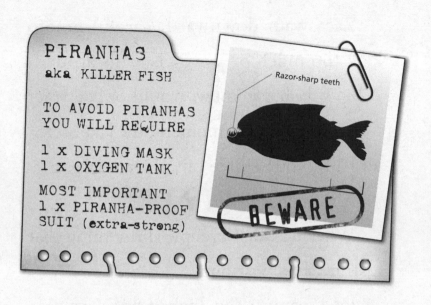

PIRANHAS
aka KILLER FISH

TO AVOID PIRANHAS
YOU WILL REQUIRE

1 x DIVING MASK
1 x OXYGEN TANK

MOST IMPORTANT
1 x PIRANHA-PROOF
SUIT (extra-strong)

Razor-sharp teeth

BEWARE

OK, Zac, he thought, *you'll just have to dive in anyway.*

He took a confident step toward the water. He stopped. *Or maybe there's another entrance to the lab somewhere else?*

But deep inside, Zac knew there wasn't. He took a huge breath and jumped in.

Zac swam downward, careful not to kick too much or wave his arms around. A big splash, he knew, would only attract the piranhas. At the moment, the lake seemed still. Not a single piranha anywhere.

Although . . . argh!

What was that creepy, slimy thing that just brushed past him?

In a panic, Zac kicked his legs. He thrashed his arms around. He screamed inside his head, *GET THAT PIRANHA AWAY FROM ME!*

He looked left. He looked right. But all there was floating near him was a gloopy clump of seaweed.

So that's what brushed against me, thought

Zac with relief. *As long as I don't make any big splashes, I'm safe.*

But even as Zac was thinking this, he realized he was still splashing around like crazy. The piranhas would find him any second! He had to swim to the bottom as fast as he could.

Down he swam at double speed.

Near the bottom, Zac saw what looked like a round door with a handle in the middle. The entrance!

Zac grabbed hold of the handle and pulled as hard as he could.

Yes! The door was heavy, but at least it was shifting. He pulled on the handle again. It was definitely coming loose! Only one more big heave and Zac would be in the lab.

Staring hard at the door, he collected every ounce of strength he had. He was just about to heave one last time when . . .

A piranha!

It swam right between Zac's face and the door, its mouth gaping open. It examined Zac's forearm. *Mmm, lunch!* it seemed to be thinking.

Desperately, Zac felt about for something to distract it. And there it was, in the pocket of his cargo pants. The entire roll of Bubble Tape with hair stuck to it! Zac broke open the pack and made a giant ball of bubble gum.

The piranha opened its terrible mouth. Its razor-sharp teeth flashed. In a second, Zac had stuffed the ball of gum into the surprised piranha's mouth.

A moment later, Zac was through the round door, through an airlock, and into Dr. Drastic's mysterious laboratory.

CHAPTER  SEVEN

What Zac found on the other side of the door was just what he expected an evil science lab to look like.

Every surface gleamed white and silver. Colored potions in glass containers bubbled and smoked over flames. Across one wall were rows and rows of tanks, all full of frogs. Each frog had a tube attached to it. Zac saw the deadly poison slowly drip,

drip, dripping up each tube and into a huge vat on the floor.

The only thing missing were the scientists. The lab was completely deserted.

Zac knew he had to work fast. He'd found one of the ingredients in Solution X—the frog poison. That was obvious. *But what were the other special ingredients mixed with the poison to create the miracle cure?*

He had to complete the formula.

Nearby, Zac saw a shelf full of books.

Zac wasn't normally that into books. But today he was. A book was just the place a complicated formula might be written down.

Zac raced over to the shelves.

He grabbed a book. *Family Recipes*, it said on the cover in curly gold writing. That looked promising. But on the first page, there was nothing but a whole lot of old-fashioned handwriting with the heading, "Mrs. Drastic's World Famous Meatloaf."

Zac was getting impatient. He had no time for Mrs. Drastic's cookbooks.

Faster and faster he searched, scanning every single book on the shelves. *101 Birthday Cakes for Evil Boys*. No good.

Tripe, Liver, & Onions—A Treasury of Horrible Treats. Yuck! No way!

Finally, Zac came to a book that was smaller than the rest. It had no title at all.

Perhaps . . .

He opened it.

This book had three formulas inside, but just like the cover, none of them had a title. Each of them listed "Frog Poison" as the first ingredient.

Suspicious, Zac thought. *Any of these recipes could be Solution X!*

Zac checked his watch.

It was 6:36 p.m.!

He needed to know which was the right recipe, and fast. There was only one way to find out: Mix up each recipe then try them all himself.

Zac rushed over to a nearby cupboard. Sure enough, it was filled with hundreds of glass bottles, each with a weird-sounding name on the label. He grabbed a crusty mixing bowl from a sink and rinsed it out.

As quickly as he could, he threw all the ingredients from the first recipe into the bowl, mixed them together, and swallowed them down.

He felt nothing. But then he saw his reflection in the bottom of a dirty saucepan. His eyes were changing color! One minute they were pink, the next they were gold, and the next they were fluorescent orange.

This couldn't be the right recipe.

He mixed up the second recipe and

swallowed that, too. Zac coughed. His cough sounded like a canary singing! Also not the right recipe.

Desperately, Zac mixed together the third recipe. He gulped it down and waited.

Nothing happened.

He checked his eyes in the saucepan. They were brown, as normal. He coughed. That sounded like a normal cough, too.

This must be it! thought Zac.

He'd found the formula for Solution X! Suddenly, a very loud grinding sound filled the lab.

Zac spun round. The entire bookshelf was turning around—it was a revolving door. Behind the bookshelf, Zac saw a dusty break room, where lab assistants sat reading magazines and drinking coffee.

And there, in the doorway, stood a pale man with cold, blue eyes and an explosion of white hair on his head. He was wearing a lab coat. Zac saw a name tag pinned to the chest.

It read, "Dr. Victor Drastic."

Dr. Drastic stuck out his hand.

"Zac Power?" he asked.

Zac's mouth dropped open in horror.

But his tongue wasn't acting like it normally did. It unrolled and unrolled and unrolled, and at the end, a whistle blew.

The third recipe had turned Zac's tongue into a party whistle!

Zac was about to be captured. And he didn't have the formula for Solution X after all!

CHAPTER ... EIGHT

"Step this way, Mr. Power," said Dr. Drastic. "Watch your head on the revolving book-case."

He was calm and polite, but icy. It was exactly how Zac's teachers sounded when someone tried the "dog ate my homework" line on them.

Zac felt Dr. Drastic's hands on his shoulders. His bony fingers and sharp fingernails dug in hard, like claws. Zac knew there was no running away from a grip like that.

"I knew you'd come sooner or later to save your brother," said Dr. Drastic. "Couldn't resist trying to make yourself a hero, could you, Zac?"

Dr. Drastic's cold, blue eyes locked with Zac's. There was something funny about the left one. Zac couldn't tell exactly what it was.

All of a sudden, Dr. Drastic reached up and popped out his left eyeball altogether.

He laid it in his palm and showed it to Zac.

"It's glass. I lost my real eye a long time ago."

Zac had never seen anything as gross as Dr. Drastic's glass eye. Unless it was the empty socket where Dr. Drastic's real eye used to be.

"Hasn't your mother ever told you it's rude to stare?" snapped Dr. Drastic. "Probably not. She's always too busy spying for GIB."

He popped his glass eye back in and Zac sighed with relief.

"I bet you hate being a spy," said Dr.

Drastic, suddenly cunning. "You'd much rather make yourself popular with your friends. Being a spy doesn't make you look cool because you can't tell anyone about it, can you?"

Zac nodded dumbly. How did Dr. Drastic know all this stuff about him? It made him feel weak and stupid all of a sudden.

So that's what they mean by an evil genius, Zac thought.

"Well, would you like to see Leon?" said Dr. Drastic. "Not to rescue him, of course. Just to say hello."

He sounded friendly again, as though he were asking Zac if he'd like a chocolate milkshake. His personality changed from nasty to friendly and back again every other minute.

It's scarier than him being horrible all the time, Zac thought.

Dr. Drastic strode over to a large silver door on the opposite side of the lab. He flung it open and inside, Zac saw Leon. But Leon wasn't standing, or even sitting with his wrists bound together with rope the way prisoners often are.

Instead, Leon was frozen inside an enormous block of ice. The expression frozen on Leon's face wasn't one of pain or fear. His forehead was wrinkled and he had a finger pressed to his cheek.

That's exactly how Leon looks when he's studying or concentrating very hard on something, thought Zac.

Dr. Drastic slammed the freezer door shut. "Don't fret, Zac," said Dr. Drastic, patting Zac's cheek creepily. "I left an air bubble in the ice block. Leon's still alive."

Relief flooded through Zac. If Leon was still alive, there was always a chance Zac could come up with some last-minute plan and save him, and maybe the formula for Solution X, too.

Zac looked around him. All the windows and doors in the lab looked really secure. Now that breaktime was over, Dr. Drastic's assistants were everywhere.

There was absolutely no way to escape. Zac's spirits sank again.

"If I don't get my money, I'm going to destroy Solution X, you see," Dr. Drastic was saying. "And while I'm at it, I thought I'd do away with Leon here, too."

Dr Drastic walked over to a model of the island in the very center of the lab.

"I'm going to drop them both into this volcano," Dr. Drastic said, pointing to a mountain on the model. A label stuck to the side read, "Mount Humble."

Zac's mind went into overdrive. He knew there was a volcano on Poison Island, but it hadn't erupted for hundreds of years.

"Ah! I see you're confused. Before

you ask, Zac—yes. You're correct. Mount Humble is an extinct volcano. Or rather, *was* an extinct volcano."

Dr. Drastic picked up a jar of powder, which looked like pepper, from a nearby bench.

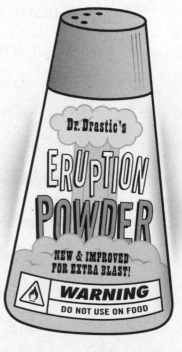

"I call my latest invention Eruption Powder. It works like pepper on a human nose. I simply sprinkle it into the crater of the extinct volcano, triggering a kind of giant, volcanic sneeze. And when the volcano's good and hot again, I'll drop in the formula for Solution X."

"Along with Leon," said Zac grimly.

"Correct!" said Dr. Drastic. "And you, too, now that you're here."

He pulled a watch on a chain from the pocket of his lab coat.

There was less than an hour until the deadline expired!

"There's a car waiting to take us to Mount Humble," said Dr. Drastic with an evil laugh. "I'm dying to hear that giant ice block sizzling in the hot lava, aren't you?"

CHAPTER NINE

Dr. Drastic's Jeep bumped along the rough jungle track toward Mount Humble. Zac's hands and feet were tied together with vines. He was squashed between Bruce and Dr. Drastic. Bradley was driving.

The giant block of ice, with Leon still frozen inside, was tied down in the back. It was late at night now, but the jungle heat was still fierce.

As sneakily as possible, Zac turned his head to get a better look at the block of ice. It seemed to be melting fast. Was it possible it might melt before they reached Mount Humble?

"Do you fancy a little car game, Zac?" asked Dr. Drastic, not waiting for an answer. "I'll start. I spy with my little eye something beginning with . . . S."

"Sweat?" said Zac, looking at Bradley's stinky, sweaty armpits. The more he played along with Dr. Drastic's stupid games, the more time he'd have to dream up a rescue strategy. He had to be careful, though. Dr. Drastic would be expecting some kind of escape attempt.

"Good try, but no," said Dr. Drastic. "S is for 'small boy trying to figure out how to rescue his brother and save the day.'"

Bruce laughed nastily and poked Zac in the ribs. Zac sighed.

"Give up, Zac. There is no escape. You won't be saving Leon. You're not getting the formula. It's O-V-E-R," said Dr. Drastic.

"That spells over," Bruce added.

At the worst possible time, Zac had really drawn a blank. He was all out of ideas!

"Look! Over there!" cried Dr. Drastic. "It's Mount Humble!"

SPYSCOPE

MOUNT HUMBLE

He clapped his hands with delight.

The Jeep turned off the main road and started climbing steadily up the side of the volcano. Before long, the Jeep stopped. Dr. Drastic got out and ordered Bradley to unload the block of ice with Leon inside.

Zac hopped along awkwardly. Walking wasn't easy with both feet tied together.

Bradley hauled the block of ice over to the very edge of the volcano crater. Bruce was busy sprinkling something into the crater itself. Dr. Drastic watched Zac with amused eyes.

"Yes, Zac. That's my Eruption Powder Bruce is sprinkling," said Dr. Drastic in his nastiest voice. He dug out his pocket watch and consulted it. "The volcano will erupt in exactly five minutes, when the deadline runs out."

Five minutes!

Things were as desperate as they had ever been.

"And when the volcano erupts, I'll have Bradley push the ice block into the lava. Then you'll follow. But since I created it, I'm going to save the pleasure of destroying Solution X for myself."

Dr. Drastic fumbled in the inside pocket of his lab coat. He pulled out a tiny jar of bright yellow liquid. "This is the last sample of Solution X," said Dr. Drastic. "I'm going to destroy this, along with the formula."

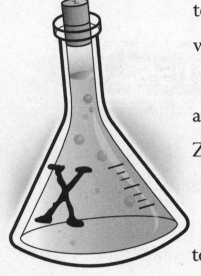

Dr. Drastic waved a piece of paper in Zac's face.

The formula!

"It makes me sad to destroy Solution X. It's my greatest invention. A cure for any disease or sickness ever known."

Dr. Drastic sighed. "It's utterly magnificent, wouldn't you say, Zac?"

But Zac wasn't listening. He was thinking about what Dr. Drastic had said. A cure for any disease or sickness ever known.

Isn't evil a kind of sickness? wondered Zac. *Is it possible that Dr. Drastic's evilness might be cured by his very own invention?*

But suddenly, Zac heard a loud gasping sound. It was coming from the volcano crater!

Ah°°° Ah°°° Ah°°°

The ground underneath him began to rumble and shake. Scalding hot steam hissed. Red-hot ash flew through the air.

Ah-choooooooo!

It was the loudest sneeze Zac had ever heard. He knew at once what was happening.

The volcano was erupting!

CHAPTER TEN

Everyone and everything anywhere near Mount Humble was trying to get away as fast as possible. Even the animals were escaping down the mountain any way they could.

But not Dr. Drastic. He stood, calm and silent, on the edge of the volcano crater. He was holding up his tiny jar of Solution X. If only Zac could get ahold of that jar!

If he was going to have any chance of that, first he'd need to break the vines that tied his wrists and ankles together. But with his hands tied together, there was no way Zac could reach his pocketknife.

Just then, Zac felt something brush up against his feet. It was a rat, trying to escape the volcano. But unlike all the other animals, this rat wasn't running. It was fat and lazy and its stomach dragged along the ground.

It was just what Zac needed!

He hopped carefully toward the rat.

Go on! Chew off those vines! he willed it.

The rat might have been lazy, but it definitely wasn't stupid. It recognized food when it saw it. It bit into the vines around Zac's ankles, then his wrists. In a few quick chews, Zac was free.

Zac snuck up behind Dr. Drastic, who was still standing on the very edge of the volcano. It would've been the easiest thing in the world to push him in. But, remembering the mission, Zac realized he couldn't. He still had to get Dr. Drastic to tell him the secret formula.

Suddenly, Dr. Drastic drew his arm back. He was about to throw his jar of Solution X into the volcano!

Zac sprang forward. He took a humongous jump. He was like a football superstar! As if in slow motion, Zac snatched the jar as it spun through midair. He cracked open the top and poured the whole bottle over Dr. Drastic!

For a second, Dr. Drastic just stood there with yellow goo dripping down his forehead. Then he spoke. His voice was nothing like the icy, terrifying voice he used before. Now, he sounded friendly but slightly confused, like a grandpa woken too early from his nap.

Bruce and Bradley rushed over to help.

"What have you done to him, you moron?" asked Bruce, looking at Zac.

"No, Bruce. That's OK. Zac's my friend!" said Dr. Drastic.

Bradley looked at Bruce, confused. This

made *no* sense to him. Bruce just shrugged his shoulders. If the boss said Zac was his friend, then Zac was his friend, as far as Bruce was concerned.

"Don't you know you're in terrible danger, Zac? We're standing on top of an erupting volcano!"

Solution X had worked! Zac had cured Dr. Drastic's evilness.

"I know," said Zac. "But I can't escape until you tell me the formula for Solution X."

"Oh, well. That's easy! To the frog poison, you simply add . . ." And he rattled off a very long list of chemicals.

Zac tried his hardest to memorize it.

He thought he had it.

"And don't forget the most important ingredient, NaCl(aq)," said Dr. Drastic. "Solution X won't work without aqueous sodium chloride—good old seawater!"

A jet of steam whooshed out of the volcano. Zac nodded. He couldn't stand around for one more second memorizing formulas. That would have to do.

"How do we escape from here, Dr. Drastic?" asked Zac.

"Take a hang glider. They're just over there. I've got plenty of spares," said Dr. Drastic.

Zac raced over to a row of hang gliders. Then he remembered Leon. How was he going to rescue his brother when he was still frozen solid in a block of ice?

He looked over at Leon. Leon was waving to him! On the side facing the volcano, the ice block had melted enough to free Leon's arm.

Zac grabbed hold of the hang glider. He took a big running start. Wind rushed under the wings. Zac was flying. **Whoosh!**

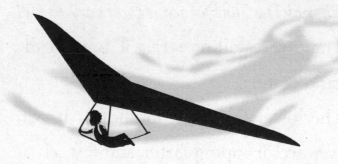

Zac circled over the volcano, then swooped back down. Leon must have understood Zac's plan perfectly.

As Zac flew overhead, Leon held his free arm up as high as he could. Zac grabbed his hand. The entire ice block lifted off the ground.

At last, Zac thought. *I've rescued Leon!*

But almost as soon as they were airborne, the hang glider began to drop downward.

Oh, no! The block of ice is too heavy to fly!

They were falling straight toward the volcano crater!

The lower they fell, the hotter it got. They were dropping faster and faster!

Leon's feet were almost in the lava.

But just when Zac thought they would surely frizzle, the hang glider suddenly rose again. Up and up it climbed, right out of the volcano crater.

Zac looked down. Flying so deep into the volcano had melted the ice block completely. Leon was free and the hang glider was light enough to fly again.

On the ground, they could just make out the tiny figure of Dr. Drastic escaping Mount Humble in one of his hang gliders. He gave Zac a friendly wave good-bye.

Zac and Leon soared away, high above Poison Island. A few minutes later, they touched down on the deck of an enormous ship. It was GIB's floating Mission Control, anchored just off the coast of Poison Island.

Zac's mom and dad were waiting for them on board.

"Mission accomplished, boys?" asked his dad proudly.

"Uh-huh," said Zac, acting cool.

His mom gave him a big sloppy kiss.

"Mom!" said Zac. *How could she be so tragic?*

The floating Mission Control was linked via satellite to the mainland HQ.

"Zac, do you have the formula for Solution X?" crackled a voice through the computer screen. It was GIB's Commander-in-Chief on the line.

"I do, Commander," he said confidently. "It's—"

Oh, no, the formula! What was it again?

Zac racked his brains. He had it! He rattled off the very long list of chemicals Dr. Drastic had added to the frog poison. Then he remembered there was one last, critical ingredient.

What was it?

"Leon?" he whispered.

"Yup?" said Leon, his lips still blue from being inside the ice block.

"I can't remember the last part of Solution X," he admitted.

"That's OK," said Leon. "While I was frozen, I studied Dr. Drastic as he was making the formula."

So that explained the look of concentration Zac had noticed on Leon's frozen face! "The last ingredient is NaCl(aq)."

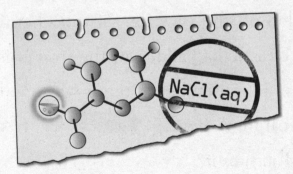

Zac was amazed.

Why hadn't he realized before how useful a geeky brother could be?

The Commander interrupted them.

"Good job, Leon. And especially well done to you, Zac," said the Commander.

Zac tried his best to look modest.

"Of course, everything you've told us about what happened on Poison Island must remain top secret. Escaping from quicksand. The cave-in. The piranha. Everything."

Zac slumped.

How boring!

"Just because you can't brag to your friends about it, it doesn't make what you've done any less important," the Commander said.

Zac thought about it.

He guessed it was true.

He'd just have to get used to being an ordinary kid for a while, doing his homework and taking Espy for walks. Still, he'd have a lot of time to practice his guitar solos. Then maybe one day he'd have thousands of fans screaming his name.

Now that, thought Zac, *really would be cool*.

... **THE END** ...